THE REMEMBERING STONE

Barbara Timberlake Russell ❖ Pictures by Claire B. Cotts

Melanie Kroupa Books ❖ Farrar, Straus and Giroux ❖ New York

To my mother, Evelyn Croley Timberlake, and my daughter, Caitlin.
Fly, Mama, while I grow wings.
—B.T.R.

To my grandmother, Florence Berman Robbins, who gave me the means
to make my wish of becoming an artist come true.
And to Melanie Kroupa, for her guidance, patience, and support in bringing this book to life.
—C.B.C.

Glossary

abuela (*ah-bwe'-la*): grandmother

abuelita (*ah-bwe-lee'-ta*): grandma

abuelo (*ah-bwe'-lo*): grandfather

Adiós por ahora (*ah-dyos' por ah-o'-ra*): Goodbye for now.

Ahora, ¡a volar! (*ah-o'-ra ah bo-lar'*): Now fly!

Buenas noches (*bwe'-nas no'-ches*): Good night.

café con leche (*ka-feh' kon leh'-che*): coffee with milk

casita (*kah-see'-ta*): little house

¡Maravilloso! (*ma-ra-beel-yo'-so*): Marvelous!

punto guanacasteco (*poon'-toh gwa-na-kas-teh'-co*): a traditional dance of Costa Rica

Que les vaya bien. (*ke les bah'-ya bee-en*): Safe journey.

Text copyright © 2004 by Barbara Timberlake Russell
Illustrations copyright © 2004 by Claire B. Cotts
All rights reserved
Distributed in Canada by Douglas & McIntyre Ltd.
Color separations by Chroma Graphics PTE Ltd.
Printed and bound in the United States of America by Berryville Graphics
Book design by Jennifer Browne
First edition, 2004
1 3 5 7 9 10 8 6 4 2

Library of Congress Cataloging-in-Publication Data
Russell, Barbara T.
    The remembering stone / by Barbara Timberlake Russell ; pictures by Claire B. Cotts.—
1st ed.
        p. cm.
    Summary: As a young girl and her mother watch the flocks of blackbirds preparing for
their journey south, the mother dreams of returning to Costa Rica where she was born.
    ISBN 0-374-36242-4
    1. Costa Rican Americans—Juvenile fiction. [1. Costa Rican Americans—Fiction.
2. Costa Rica—Fiction. 3. Mothers and daughters—Fiction. 4. Dreams—Fiction.] I. Cotts,
Claire, ill. II. Title.

PZ7.R91536 Re 2004
[E]—dc21
                                                                                2002074228

In early fall, the blackbirds creak like rusty wheels behind our apartment. My mother tells me they are calling us outside, asking us to share our breakfast of white coffee and banana bread.

"Imagine the places they go, Ana," Mamá tells me. "The things they see."

As we walk into the garden, they lift like a carpet being shaken, then fall again in one piece, as if the carpet has been laid out to air in the sun.

We bring scraps of bread and cooked rice for the birds. Mamá says they only stop here to rest before continuing their long trip.

"Maybe this time they will fly far across the ocean," my mother says. She raises her face toward the sky and fingers the locket at her neck.

I know what she is thinking. Inside the locket is a picture of my grandmother and grandfather far away in Costa Rica, where Mamá was born.

"One day I will return like you," my mother tells the birds. "But for now, you go. *Que les vaya bien.* Safe journey."

Sometimes, before the birds fly away, my mother opens the locket and shows me the picture of her *mamá* and *papá*. She has told me stories of volcanoes that rise like a spine down the center of her country, and of the herds of cattle her brothers and father drive onto the green mountain slopes.

She never takes the locket off, she says, because it reminds her of her dream of going home.

My best friend, Sophia, has a dream, too. She wants to be
a great actress. Me, I'm not sure what my dream is. For now,
I make up stories and act them out with Sophia when Mamá
goes to work.

Mrs. Pettibone, my friend next door, claps when we finish.
She tells us her wish. "One day I will no longer rent this old
place. I will own it." Then she throws dirt from the window
box over her shoulder. "It takes luck to make a dream come true."

While we eat lunch, Sophia tells Mr. Nguyen that she dreams of being an actress.

"Someday I will bring my family here to live, that is my dream," Mr. Nguyen says. "Then we will all be together again. But for now, I must save money and hold hope inside me." As the bell on the counter rings, he says, "Most fragile things, these dreams."

After lunch, Sophia and I stop to watch Pockets dancing in front of a blanket lined with coins.

"Actress, you say?" Pockets scratches his chin. He slides the toe of his shoe along the ground in a wide semicircle. Suddenly his feet spring into a series of taps and shuffles, making music on the sidewalk.

We applaud and Pockets bows low.

"Work hard, my friends," he says. "That's how you make dreams come true."

After we say goodbye, Sophia and I walk to the bakery where Mamá works. "To be an actress," Sophia says, "you must study how people move and talk."

Mamá leans over the counter, her fingers resting lightly as a piano player's against the glass. Her dark hair glistens. She reminds me of the first bird that came into our garden this morning.

We crouch down low so we can watch Mr. Hoffer, who owns the bakery. He mixes bread dough in the kitchen. Mr. Hoffer never smiles. Even his eyes seem angry, and his hands, too, as he pinches off pieces of dough to make into rolls.

When he spots us, he shakes his fist. "Can't you kids find anything better to do than snoop?"

"We're not snooping, we're watching people," I tell him, "so Sophia can be a great actress."

"Ha! You think just because you want something you can have it?" Mr. Hoffer pounds his floured fist into a mound of dough and we race down the sidewalk.

That night, I tell my mother that Mr. Hoffer reminds me
of a camel, because camels are bad-tempered all the time, too.
    My mother cocks her head. "Poor Mr. Hoffer," she says. "He
has forgotten that a person must have dreams as well as bread."
    Tomorrow I will write down the stories I made up for
Sophia. Then she won't forget her dream and end up angry like
Mr. Hoffer.

"I think that if I could be any animal in the world," I tell
my mother, "I would be a blackbird, like the ones in our garden."
"Then you could fly to Costa Rica and come home to tell me
all you saw," Mamá said.

She throws my blanket over my head and lets it settle over
me like a cloud. "*Buenas noches*, little bird," she calls from the door.

When Mamá leaves, I slip out of bed and lift down the box from Costa Rica. It holds a fan and a straw doll and some letters, but my favorite thing is a stone, black with yellow and red flecks that cross near the center.

When she gave it to me, Mamá said, "This is a stone spit from the great volcanoes in Costa Rica. I brought it with me to help me remember, like the picture of your grandparents in my locket."

Down the hallway, I hear my mother singing softly. I put the box away before I get back in bed, but I keep the stone under my pillow, where I can touch it. I close my eyes and imagine the land from which it came.

I think that maybe, just for tonight, I will be a bird.

My black feathers spread as I rise toward the stars. Across my wings is a fan of red and yellow. Like the colors of that first bird that hopped into the garden this morning. Like the stone under my pillow.

I fly straight south, where ships cut into the silver line of the horizon. Shadows move under the waves. Storms send down curtains of rain.

At last I reach land, the
shores of Costa Rica. Mountains
stretch over steamy cedar and ebony
forests, noisy with bright birds. Coffee trees
blossom. The scent of ripe bananas and sugar mills
mixes with the ocean breezes. And there, beyond
Puntarenas, lies my grandparents' house.

I see my grandfather and uncles gathering cacao pods from the trees. As I fly closer, I can smell rice and beans and the hot peppers my grandmother fries for their dinner. Finally, my wings touch the dark green leaves that grow outside the window of my grandparents' *casita*.

I watch my grandmother as she cooks. She sings the way Mamá does when she thinks no one is listening. From Mamá's pictures, I recognize the hand-painted brick oven Abuela made and the table Abuelo carved. I spot a picture under the cross that hangs on the wall, a photograph of Mamá and me.

When I see the two of us here in this house, so far away from our own apartment in the city, something inside me lifts as though it has only been resting for the long journey home. Suddenly I, too, want to sing so that I can be heard far across the sea.

And then I know. One day, Mamá, you and I will come to Puntarenas together.

We will stay in this house of my grandmother
and grandfather and uncles, and we will all hug
until our arms are tired from squeezing.

We will sit in metal chairs at the water's edge and drink *café con leche* and eat my grandmother's tortillas. And in celebration, my uncles will dance the *punto guanacasteco*. Then I will write down everything I see and hear so that I will always remember.

But for now, darkness folds around me. It is late.

"*Adiós por ahora, Abuelita y Abuelo,*" I whisper as I rise into the night. High above the sea, I search the land below. My grandparents' house becomes only a dot in a carpet of black.

When I open my eyes, I touch the stone, cool under my pillow. I take my notebook from under my bed and begin to write all that I remember about my dream. Mamá appears in the doorway dressed for work. I want to tell her that I have heard Abuela sing in her warbly voice and that I have seen Abuelo with his hat pulled down low on his forehead. But instead I only say, "Mamá, I have had the best dream."

"*¡Maravilloso!*" My mother smiles and kisses me. "But hurry now. Our friends are coming."

When the first blackbird flies down and lands at the spread of crumbs and rice on the grass, we smile and sip our *café con leche*. In a moment, the yard is covered with bobbing heads.

My hands are cold. When I stuff them in my jacket I feel the stone I took from under my pillow and placed in my pocket. I will put it there every day, keep it with me. I will wish for luck, work hard, and hold hope inside, till my dream comes true.

My mother touches the cross on her locket as the birds begin to flutter. "They're leaving."

A rustling of wings brings us to our feet. Mamá takes my hand.

Suddenly, I cannot wait to begin the journey. I throw my arms high. *"Ahora, ¡a volar!"* I shout. "Fly!" And feel myself lift to my toes—as the sea of birds leaps for the sun.